W9-DJA-930

Through the Eyes of CHILDREN

EGYPT

Connie Bickman

Published by Abdo & Daughters, 4940 Viking Drive, Suite 622, Edina, Minnesota 55435.

Printed in the United States.

Cover Photo credit: Connie Bickman
Interior Photo credits: Connie Bickman

Edited by Julie Berg

LIBRARY OF CONGRESS CATALOGING-IN-PUBLICATION DATA

Bickman, Connie
    Egypt / Connie Bickman.
      p. cm. -- (Through the eyes of children)
    Includes Index.
    Summary: Introduces the people, food, clothing, dwellings, schools work, and other aspects of life in Egypt.
    ISBN 1-56239-548-3 (lib. bdg.)
    1. Children -- Egypt -- Social life and customs -- Juvenile Literature.
    2. Egypt -- Social life and customs -- Juvenile literature. [1. Egypt-- Social life and customs.] I. Title. II. Series.
    DT70.353 1996
    962--dc20   98-38849
                                    CIP
                                    AC

Contents

Welcome to Egypt!

Egypt is an ancient country.
Its history is filled with pharaohs, kings and mighty rulers.
Cleopatra reigned as queen in the city of Alexandria.
Baby Moses was found on the Nile River.
The country is historic, religious, and mysterious.

Egypt is famous for the pyramids, the Great Sphinx, and beautiful temples.
Temple walls are covered with paintings and writings.
There are hieroglyphs that tell stories of the past.
Some of these stories are called mythology.
They tell of people who turned into falcons or dog-headed gods.
Some told of the everyday lives of the people who lived there.

The Valley of the Kings also tells of Egypt's history.
Many Egyptian rulers are buried there.
Also buried in their tombs were treasures and gold.
A mask of King Tutankhamon is made of pure gold.
He was only 18 years old when he died.
A collection of treasures from his tomb is in the Egyptian Museum in Cairo.

Egypt is part of Africa.
But it is very different from most other African countries. Egypt has a great influence of Arabian culture and religion.
Most Arabs are Muslim.
They follow Islamic teachings.

The Nile River is important to the Egyptian people. Ninety-five percent of the population lives along the Nile. The river flows south to north into the Mediterranean Sea. It begins in Tanzania, flowing up through Uganda and Sudan.

Egypt is divided into two parts.
The northern fourth of the country is called Lower Egypt.
The southern three-fourths of the land is called Upper Egypt.
Within Sudan is a region called Nubia, from which many ancient Egyptians came.

The Mediterranean Sea borders Egypt on the north.
The Red Sea is on the east.
Egypt's borders reach through the Sinai Peninsula and touch Israel.
African borders are Libya and Sudan.
Egypt has many neighbors!

Detail area

THE
MIDDLE
EAST

EGYPT

Mediterranean Sea

Israel

Lower
Egypt

Sinai
Peninsula

Upper
Egypt

Red
Sea

L
i
b
y
a

EGYPT

N U B I A

Sudan

Meet the Children

You will enjoy the children of Egypt.
They are very friendly and enjoy talking with visitors.
Most of the children speak English.
But the official language is Arabic.

There are three main ethnic groups in Egypt:
The descendants of ancient Egyptians, Arabs, and Nubians.
Nubians live in Southern Egypt.
They came from Sudan.

The Egyptian population is over 55 million.
There are a lot of children to play with in this small country!
Let's meet the children of Egypt.

What Do They Eat?

This boy is buying sweet potatoes in an outdoor market.
The market is called a souk.
Fruit and vegetables are sold fresh every day.
A scale weighs the food to see how much it costs.

Children roast corn cobs on an open fire.
They are careful not to burn themselves.
For dessert they will have pudding.
It is called mahalabya.
It is ground rice with milk and sugar.
Sometimes dried grapes and peanuts are added.

This boy is having fun at the market. He is selling beans and potatoes. Beans mixed with olive oil is a popular dish. Sugarcane, millet, beans, rice, and onions are also grown in Egypt. Dried fruits, like dates, are favorite foods.

Fresh bread is sold every day in the markets.
It is baked over coals in stone ovens.
You can buy the flat, round bread while it is still warm.
Delicious pastries like baklava are favorites.
Baklava is filo dough, drizzled with honey and nuts.

What Do They Wear?

Egyptian girls usually wear dresses or skirts. Sometimes they wear very modern clothes. Sometimes they wear long, traditional dresses. Veils are worn as part of the Islamic religion, and as protection from the hot sun.

Special occasion dresses can also be modern or traditional. This girl is wearing a costume with jewels and embroidery. It is her family's custom to dress in traditional clothing.

Boys wear flowing robes of blue or white just like their fathers do.

These robes are called galabeya.

They are made of cotton and are very cool when it is hot outside. Some boys wear trousers and shirts or shorts and T-shirts. Not many boys wear jeans because the weather is too warm.

Where Do They Live?

Over half of all Egyptians live in villages along the Nile River.
They also use the river for transportation.
Their houses are built from sun-dried mud bricks.
City dwellers live in houses or high-rise city apartments.

Some people are fellahin, or farmers.
They grow their own food and they fish in the Nile River.

Some bedouin families live in goat-haired tents
in the Sahara or Arabian deserts.
Bedouins are goat and camel herders.
They are also nomadic.
That means they move around to find food for their
grazing animals.
Some bedouin families settle in permanent towns.
Unlike traditional bedouin families, they live a modern
lifestyle.

Getting Around

Camels carry people and goods over the desert and in the city.

Trains, cars and buses are also used.

There are no super highways so it may take a long time to travel through the countryside.

You will often have to wait because there are animals on the road!

Donkeys pull carts through the busy city traffic.

On crowded city streets you will see cars alongside donkey carts and camels.

People travel the Nile by boat.
Ships, motor boats and flat barges are common.
Feluccas are traditional sailboats used on the river.

School is Fun!

These children are up early in the morning for school.
They have been playing soccer.
Some wear traditional robes to school.
Some wear modern clothing.

In Lower Egypt, children ages 6 to 19 must go to
school.
Students then can attend one of the six universities.
For primary grades there are free government schools
and private schools.
In Upper Egypt there are few schools, and
no education laws for children.
Many children are needed to farm the land.
About half of Egypt's population cannot read or write.

How Do They Work?

These children are delivering fresh bakery goods to the market and to local restaurants.

They must get up early every day while the breads are fresh.

You must have good balance to carry bread trays on your head.

Children often sell clothing, fabric, and baskets.
It may be hot during the day and sometimes business
is slow.
But this boy likes to visit with the people who pass by.
He is a good salesman.

Their Land

The pyramids of Giza are in Egypt.
They were built when pharaohs ruled the land.
There are nine pyramids at Giza.
The three largest pyramids are Cheops, Chephren, and Micerinus.
They were built for pharaohs Khufu, Khafre, and Menkure.
There are many other pyramids in the Egyptian deserts.
They are tombs for ancient Egyptian rulers.
The Great Sphinx lies in front of the Pyramid of Cheops.
It has a lion's body and a human head.

Temples with enormous stone columns are everywhere in Egypt.
Luxor, Karnac, Edfu, and Abu Simbel are a few of them.
The walls and columns are covered with hieroglyphics.
They are ancient writings that tell of the land's history.
Hieroglyphics are shown in inscriptions and in pictures.

Life in the City

Cairo is Africa's largest city.
It is Egypt's capital.
Over 15 million people live there.
Cairo's streets are always crowded.
Car horns honk all the time and people are always rushing.
It is a very modern city with a mix of old and new.
Khan al-Khalili Bazaar has modern shops in ancient buildings.

The Mosque of Mohammed Ali in Cairo is sacred for the people of Islam.
It was built by Mohammed Ali Pasha, an Egyptian governor.
The mosque has a domed roof and tall minarets that can be seen from almost anywhere in the city.
Minarets are high towers.
Prayers are sung from them every day.
Call-to-prayer is chanted through loud-speakers five times a day.
Every time prayer is called, the Moslem people kneel to pray, facing towards Mecca.
Mecca is the holy city in Saudi Arabia.
It is the homeland of Islam, the birthplace of Mohammed.
Mohammed was a prophet, the founder of the Islamic religion.

Family Life

Family life is important in Egypt.
Young children spend most of their time with family.
They are often with their mothers as they work.
This child and her mother are coming from the market. Balancing heavy bundles on her head is common for an Egyptian woman.

In some households, children live with their parents and grandparents.
Cousins, aunts and uncles often live close by.
This closeness creates strong family ties.
Children usually get much attention with so many relatives nearby.
This family is on a holiday, visiting the temple of Karnac.

Children are the Same

It is fun to see how children in other countries live. Children may play and go to school and have families just like you.

They may work, travel, and dress differently than you.

One thing is always the same.

That is a smile. If you smile at other children, they will smile back.

That is how you make new friends.

It is fun to have new friends all over the world!

Glossary

Abu Simbel (a-boo SIM-bel) - a temple in the Nubian Desert with gigantic statues of pharaohs.

Arabic (AIR-a-bic) - official language of Egypt.

Baklava (bahk-LAH-vah) - a flakey pastry.

Bedouin (BED-o-win) - a nomadic Arab.

Delta (DEL-tah)- wetlands from a nearby body of water.

Edfu (ED-fu)- the most preserved temple in Egypt.

Ethnic (ETH-nic) - culture, or race, of a people.

Fellahin (fell-A-hin) - farmers of the Nile River Valley.

Feluccas (fell-OO-caz) - sailboats on the Nile River.

Galabeya (GALA-beya) - long cotton gowns worn in Egypt.

Great Pyramids of Giza - gigantic pyramids near Cairo that were built as tombs for pharaohs.

Great Sphinx - a statue with a lion's body and a human's head.

Hieroglyphics (hi-ro-GLYPH-ics) - paintings and writings that tell about the past.

Islam (IS-lam) - religion of the Moslem people.

Karnak (KAR-nak) - the temple of Amon in Karnak is the largest temple in the world supported by columns.

Khan al-Khalili Bazaar (khan al-kha-LI-li) - one of the main marketplaces in Cairo with many ancient buildings.

King Tutankhamon (toot-tan-KAW-mon) - a young king (King Tut) who ruled for a short period of time.

Luxor (LUX-or) - for centuries it was the capitol of the Egyptian Kingdom.

Mahalabya (ma-HALL-a-bah) - a pudding made from rice, milk, and sugar.

Mecca (MEC-aw) - a holy city in Saudi Arabia, the birthplace of Mohammed.

Muslim (MUZ-lim) - a believer in the Islamic religion.

Mythology (myth-OL-ogy) - mystical legends or stories.

Nomadic (no-MAD-ic) - people who move their homes (usually tents) from one place to another.

Nubian (NU-bi-an) - ethnic group in Egypt who came from Sudan.

Pharaoh (PHAR-oh) - king.

Pharaohs Khugu (KU-gu), **Khafre** (KAF-ree), and **Menkure** (MEN-kure) - Pharoahs or Kings of Egypt.

Pyramid of Cheops (CHE-ops) - the largest of the pyramids at Giza.

Pyramid of Chephren (CHEF-ren) - the second largest of the pyramids at Giza.

Pyramid of Micerimus (mic-er-E-mus) - the third largest of the pyramids at Giza.

Souk - marketplace.

Valley of the Kings - a place in the desert where Egyptian kings and rulers are buried.

whirling dervish (DER-vish) - a traditional dancer, usually a male.

Index

About the Author/Photographer

Connie Bickman is a photojournalist whose photography has won regional and international awards.

She is retired from a ten-year newspaper career and currently owns her own portrait studio and art gallery. She also is an active freelance photographer and writer who travels the far corners of the world to photograph native cultures.

Connie is a member of the National Press Association and the Minnesota Newspaper Photographers Association.